Note to parents, carers and teachers

Read it yourself is a series of modern stories, favourite characters and traditional tales written in a simple way for children who are learning to read. The books can be read independently or as part of a guided reading session.

Each book is carefully structured to include many high-frequency words vital for first reading. The sentences on each page are supported closely by pictures to help with understanding, and to offer lively details to talk about.

The books are graded into four levels that progressively introduce wider vocabulary and longer stories as a reader's ability and confidence grows.

Ideas for use

- Begin by looking through the book and talking about the pictures. Has your child heard this story before?

- Help your child with any words he does not know, either by helping him to sound them out or supplying them yourself.

- Developing readers can be concentrating so hard on the words that they sometimes don't fully grasp the meaning of what they're reading. Answering the puzzle questions at the end of the book will help with understanding.

For more information and advice on Read it yourself and book banding, visit **www.ladybird.com/readityourself**

Book Band

6

Level 2 is ideal for children who have received some reading instruction and can read short, simple sentences with help.

Special features:

Frequent repetition of main story words and phrases

Short, simple sentences

Large, clear type

Careful match between story and pictures

Topsy and Tim were twins. They were going to London for the first time.

6

7

First, Topsy and Tim went to see the Tower of London.

"It looks like a castle," said Tim.

8

9

Educational Consultant: Geraldine Taylor
Book Banding Consultant: Kate Ruttle

Written by Ellen Philpott
Illustrated by Belinda Worsley

A catalogue record for this book is available from the British Library

Published by Ladybird Books Ltd
80 Strand, London, WC2R 0RL
A Penguin Company

007

ISBN: 978-0-72329-086-5

Printed in China

Topsy and Tim
Go to London

By Jean and Gareth Adamson

Topsy and Tim were twins.
They were going to London
for the first time.

First, Topsy and Tim went to see the Tower of London.

"It looks like a castle," said Tim.

The twins liked the Tower of London. It was a great castle to play in.

The next day, Topsy and Tim
went on an underground
train. They had to go down
and down underground
to get to the train.

Dad said they were
going to see a parade.

13

The parade was great.

"The horses look very big,"
said Tim.

"Horses are great,"
said Topsy.

14

The next day, Topsy and Tim went on a boat.

"I can see a big clock," said Topsy.

"I saw it first," said Tim.

"That clock is Big Ben," said Mummy.

The boat went to some gardens. Topsy and Tim ran about and played. They went up in the trees, too.

The next day, Topsy and Tim went to a museum. It had some big model dinosaurs.

"This is a great museum," said Topsy.

"I like it too," said Tim.

Just then, one of the dinosaurs made a big ROAR!

"Ooh!" said Topsy.

"That roar made me jump!" said Tim.

Mummy said it was just a model.

The next day, Topsy and
Tim went to a garden.
It was a very good
garden to play in.

"Look at this big
boat!" said Tim.

Then Dad saw a statue. Topsy and Tim went over to it. Just then, the statue looked up!

"Ooh, that made me jump!" said Topsy.

"It's a man being a statue," said Tim.

Then it was time for Topsy and Tim to go home.

"London is great," said Tim.

"It's great being home too," said Topsy.

How much do you remember about the story of Topsy and Tim: Go to London? Answer these questions and find out!

- What does Tim think the Tower of London looks like?

- What kind of train do Topsy and Tim go on?

- Which big clock do Topsy and Tim see from the boat?

- What makes Tim jump at the museum?

Look at the pictures and match them
to the story words.

Topsy

Tim

Dad

Mummy

boat

dinosaur

Read it yourself with Ladybird

Tick the books you've read!

For beginner readers who can read short, simple sentences with help.

Level 2

Beauty and the Beast ☐
Chicken Licken ☐
Rumpelstiltskin ☐
Sleeping Beauty ☐
The Gingerbread Man ☐
Dom's Dragon ☐

Little Red Riding Hood ☐
Nature Trail ☐
Sports Day ☐
Pirate School ☐
Sly Fox and Red Hen ☐
The Tale of Jemima Puddle-Duck ☐
The Three Little Pigs ☐
Why Lion Roarrrs! ☐

The Big Race ☐
Town Mouse and Country Mouse ☐
School Bus Trip ☐
Topsy and Tim Go to London ☐
The Princess and the Frog ☐
Treehouse Rescue ☐

For more confident readers who can read simple stories with help.

Level 3

You won't like this present as much as I DO! ☐
The Elves and the Shoemaker ☐
Hansel and Gretel ☐
Harry and the Bucketful of Dinosaurs ☐
Jack and the Beanstalk ☐
The Red Knight ☐

Furi on Music Island ☐
Popper Stows Away ☐
Rapunzel ☐
Aladdin ☐
The Jungle Book ☐
Roxy and the Great Escape ☐
Angry Birds Cheer up Chuck! ☐
Angry Birds Bomb's Best Birthday ☐